WHERE YOU ARE?

NINGTHOUJAM BASANTA SINGH

BLUEROSE PUBLISHERS
India | U.K.

Copyright © Ningthoujam Basanta Singh 2024

All rights reserved by author. No part of this publication may be reproduced, stored in a retrieval system or transmitted in any form or by any means, electronic, mechanical, photocopying, recording or otherwise, without the prior permission of the author. Although every precaution has been taken to verify the accuracy of the information contained herein, the publisher assumes no responsibility for any errors or omissions. No liability is assumed for damages that may result from the use of information contained within.

BlueRose Publishers takes no responsibility for any damages, losses, or liabilities that may arise from the use or misuse of the information, products, or services provided in this publication.

For permissions requests or inquiries regarding this publication, please contact:

BLUEROSE PUBLISHERS
www.BlueRoseONE.com
info@bluerosepublishers.com
+91 8882 898 898
+4407342408967

ISBN: 978-93-6452-772-9

Cover Design: Sadhna Kumari
Typesetting: Pooja Sharma

First Edition: August 2024

PREFACE

I write this book to encourage and inspire the people to achieve their goals. Goalless people dies carrying his dream into grave. Everybody has his own creative genius and however, it is difficult to find his appropriate genius. So you need to find what you love most in life.

I went through many phases of life's changes. Change in inevitable. I was not very excellent in academic career. But I am a talented person.

In the way of my living I didn't have any goal. This is the main hurdle in the progress of my life.

After reading many books on motivation I came to know that is essential to keep a big goal in life.

In the way of my life I had many experience from very bad to good ones. Now money is my problem. I need money very much. I know that money is very important in my living. For this I would like to appreciate Barry Farber, whose book was the first to inspire me. I would like to thank to PANTHOU and Amway and My wife.

Further, I am not an expert in the field of writing, nothing is my new invention. It is the mixture of ideas from the books I read, some of my experience in the field of business as my career. I am a learner of business I want to share my experience in the development of my living, life style by adapting in the first changing world and lead to a good life.

You, the reader can be what you want to be in life, you can reach at the top of the world.

Now, I would like to thank the Blue Rose Publisher for inspiration to write this little book; to share my story helping people to reach their goal of lives.

To my observations, scientific knowledge and arts should go together. Arts builds theories, creativity, hypothesis and metaphysical, while science creates and investigates, dissect and re dissect any things under investigation. They are so correlated. The trend is that science goes separately from Arts.

Actually they should go together for the advancement of humanity and Three Rs are a must. Writing, reading and arithmetic's for everybody.

CONTENTS

1. FINANCIAL FREEDOM 1
2. INNER STRENGH 4
3. FRIENDS, NEIGHBOURS, RELATIVE AND FAMILY HARMONY 8
4. HEALTH AND SOUND MIND 12
5. CREATIVITY 15
6. PROFESSION 19
7. FAME 22
8. SAVING 24
9. TIME MANAGEMENT 27
CONCLUSION 29
ABOUT THE BOOK 32

Chapter –I

FINANCIAL FREEDOM

I started my life in the low living conditions. I was not good in how to earn money. Anyway I was good in gambling carom and play chess. I earned my expenditure by gambling carom. I also started earning money by painting, gift cards painting, no. Plating on cars, on two wheelers and also earned my living by taking tuition for small kids.

However, it was not sufficient to build my new life. One of the reason I got late marriage was money discrepancy. So money was my thought, I thought money and money.

Suddenly by chance I came across a book written by Drew Farber at Guwahati Train station. I did not know it was good book and later it inspired me highly. From the display of books at the train station, I took (picked it) up at random. I read it many times.

Afterwards I started to seek inspirational books, it was because of financial freedom to be achieved.

Financial freedom does not mean to acquire huge wealth such as owning big hotels, big company, hospital etc. I mean by financial freedom is a life living in abundance, where you can do, eat ,live, buy whatever you need accordingly.

So, I really feel it is business that can you free from unhappy life, financial tension.

I suggest you to do business is to achieve freedom of speech, freedom of finance. Do business on trial and learning basis. Never invest whatever you have. Business requires learning and experience. When you have experience naturally you will be able to handle your business. So I would suggest you to join first in others business set up, learn how they are doing their business. What I mean is that without experience I started my business where I failed many times but I didn't fall back because I invested a little amount of money, from that failure I got lesson but I lost money, my time, however I could survive anyhow since I was resilient. So do little investment for setback to comeback.

Choosing of wrong trades with little knowledge of it made my failure. Be tenacious, be perseverance in the field you are doing. These are important elements in business. Be resilient and choose your right trade. You do it, follow it, you will be financially free.

One of the best for learning business is to join first in shops, factory, company etc. and work as a salesman, worker. You will learn anything that requires in running a business apart. Then try to build your own.

When you own your business, still you need to adapt the changes. Change is inevitable, accept change you will achieve your success and happiness and financial freedom. However success is not a destination, it is a journey of life. Success after success, now you will be free and happy.

Everybody wants financial freedom but they don't know how to get. I advise you readers to just start any profession, any jobs, any work, farms, shoe making, bee keeping, selling, painting, smith, music, film role. It is your happiness with what you are doing, the success.

Now learn more, know more and earn more you will be happy. Money is absolutely all so to say, it is the way now you use money that makes you unhappy, it is the way you use the money to make you happy.

Money you seek for your happiness. Definitely earning money and your happiness require your inner strength.

Very intriguing question is that why we are poor and other become rich.

Now, you see nature is perfectly moulded. Blind people has specially developed intelligence in certain areas, they are skilled in singing. writing, playing musical instrument example. Beethoven who was deaf but was skilled in piano playing.

Now, that above! we poor people ! That we all are constructed on hierarchical and developmental steps, promotions. But chaos is brought by breaking this hierarchy of nature's systems.

Never blame you as well as your past mistakes it is you and we, who are responsible for our faults.

Don't worry we will stand on the top of the world, because poor are blessed for them there is an opportunity to emulate and develop their lives' woes.

Chapter - II

INNER STRENGH

Emotions havoc us. Controlling emotions requires inner strength. This is very important part of the success in live and in business.

Inner strength does not mean only controlling your emotions. It also means spirituality in your capacity to do on moral and ethics.

Inner strength requires your will, very important part of the success of your business. Handling of Ego is a milestone in the part of the journey of life, your happiness.

I use concentration, meditation to control my mind and to focus on the subject under hand. It requires daily practice at least five to fifteen minutes.

You can do it in the morning when you wake up or in the night before bed time. You can visualize what you want to achieve particularly your business. Start just today. Don't fear whatever it comes in your mind, let it go free and try to connect with your goals in hand in your thinking during meditation.

I mention here goal because without goal a life is meaning less.

Concentration and meditation is for controlling your mind. Your body follows your mind.

Mind never allows vacuum. I used fill up the vacuum by chanting or refilling it by the words what I want with my goals in life.

For example I say to myself "I am happy, I am healthy and wealthy and beautiful" so it will work definitely. I call this is to elevate inner strength. I want to mean it as spirituality, inner power to do work on morality. Now, think and say words according to your desire, like I did, practice it. It will give your inner strength. When you give to it regularly you will grow your inner strength. You will be able to change quickly your bad habits into a good one. Bad habit is because we don't know what life is meant. We are born for something. We are meant to be something on this earth. We all become the victim of bad habits. It is because we all are attracted toward pleasure habits. If you are goal oriented and have good inner strength you will definitely change quickly into good ones. Pleasure habits will become your play thing.

The more you grow your inner strength you will get tranquility and happiness of life.

The test of your inner strength will come to you definitely. Try to control your emotions. You cannot eliminate emotions such as anger, hatred, jealousy, love, envy, joy etc.

They are eternal part of your life. The only thing you can do is to control them, keep them in check and balance.

When you grow people will feel jealous of you. They will start to check and see your faults. Never mind, jealousy is part of human emotions. It is you who should strengthen your inner strength. Think everything positively. Reason it, develop more power from inside. Your inside is your real power. Your inside is real you who you are.

I do it, I practice it, I can it. I succeed to grow my inner strength to be calm, happy and then success. You will be able to face problems of life by taking out more inner power.

You do it which I can do. Do it now your mind is your friend and control your mind by daily practice of meditation. Develop your inner power.

Yes, right, you may face environment problems. See now chapter III, your environment, friends, family and society.

Inner Strength depends on your habits (bad habits and good habits) you are the product of the amount of foods and its quality and behavior (work done by you). Habits play a very great role in what you are and you will be. When you control you and when you change quickly what you were anytime, any day you are the master of your mind and master of your destiny. Nobody can pull you down.

Nowadays things change quickly, try to adapt the change by your inner strength.

Among habits the worst is that kill you slowly, example is smoking. Habit of sex is your last encounter.

Take deep meditation. Don't stop asking 'how' where, why and what

Your mind is your world. It acts in various different way. Mind never allows to be in vacuum. It is how you handle your mind that makes what you are.

You encounter problems Yes, really life is full of problems. Encounter it, face it -problem of finance, family friends, society. But you are free when ethics and morality rules you.

Chapter-III

FRIENDS, NEIGHBOURS, RELATIVE AND FAMILY HARMONY

Every chapter is equally important in attaining success in life. Your goal, your dream is for your success. No goal, no success. Opportunity is surrounding you. It is you who cannot capture that opportunity.

People are growing in number every day so different activities are being done day by day. Their activities may be good or may be bad.

Now your concern is to make success. Your activities should be orchestrated with activities conducive to your success.

People is your environment. Your success depends on them. Make touch with friends, make touch with your family.

The best way is harmonious living with friends, family, neighbors. They form what we call society.

Friends are good customers. Try to connect frequently with them. Frequently give them love, gifts that you can. Same is also for family and relatives. They are good supporters of you, constant touch with them is good in your progress. Accept them, appreciate them.

Feel them important to you and let they feel you important. Everybody likes love, appreciation, give what you can to them, love, appreciation. It does not mean giving all you have.

Some of your colleagues, neighbour etc. may feel jealous of your progress. Don't mind. It is natural. Try to teach them how to grow and explain how you encountered difficulties in attaining your success. Help them to grow. It is your duty.

On my part, I care my family, my wife and my employees, they are happy with me. Also I did help friends.

My wife is body and I am the mind. 60 p.c. of my work is taken charge by my wife.

So please think of it !

Now, yes, during pandemic I met difficulties in my business. I have the burden of interest for the money I borrowed for my business. But I did business.

I connected to all my friend customers during first pandemic wave. I delivered them foods and other items whatever they demanded from my company.

Thus I could save my burden of interest. This means I earned during 1st Pandemic of Covid-19. Verily, I myself as a trader went to distribute to meet my customers' wants.

I am happy. I was exhausted but I was happy during those days. It was because I did them with joy.

So, you do everything you want with joy and enthusiasm. You will be successful and happy.

Therefore, friends, family, neighbours, locality of your state are your environment. Try to develop the highest good relations.

Ignore any bad comments, avoid somebody down pulling you, use your intelligence rightly. To face difficulties and hardship, challenges are natural part in the way to success. You love them, never fail to love them. It will return to you in direct or either in unseen form. It is your duty to make them happy and you to be loved by them. Example, you may be singer, right, you sing songs to the extent of giving joy to them by your performance.

This is the best way. This is your duty. The same is also true in other areas.

Mike Tyson fought, he was great because he fought for excitement and happiness for the audiences.

As you continue reading my book you find that your success is very much related with your harmonious, co-ordinative relations with your family, friends and neighbours - so called your environment.

You also see that without health you can cannot enjoy life, without good health you cannot be successful. Even though you are successful you cannot enjoy life without good health.

On another side, I am the mind, she is my body. Most of my work was worked out through my wife. Most of my work was worked out through my friends. It is almost impossible to reach my abundance without her and my friends. Women are very important in the part of success journey. Same is true for women also.

Many people don't use this power. If you start your own business whether big or small the role of women is very important.

Time change now, situations also change, old thinking of husband earns and wife to be housewife is no longer good idea.

Chapter - IV

HEALTH AND SOUND MIND

Health is everything, without good health you cannot have good mind. Without good mind your health will not be good. Mind and body are so intricately connected. Mind spread throughout the body, any scratch on your hand or legs, two extremities of your body you will feel pain. It is through mind. Mind is the commander and body, the follower of this commander. So good mind means good body.

Without good health you cannot do your work efficiently. Now you work hard. You earn lots money but you cannot enjoy the money because of bad health.

So body and mind should be developed by proper practice.

Try to think good thoughts your body will follow. Good thoughts should be based on morality and ethics.

Well, all of us require to have goals, all goals should go in concert. These means that health goals, money goals, family and society goals, saving goals and time management goals, all must be coordinated and concerted.

Body is consisted head where your brain, eyes, years, nose mouth is located. Then neck is where important thyroid is located. Through neck all foods you eat carried down to stomach. Through nose you carry down oxygen. Other parts of body are equally important. You need to take care of them. Say chest, belly, trunk. legs and hands.

Take exercise to improve all parts of your body. Some don't take care of hands and legs. You should avoid to neglect hands and legs. Keep them good with proper exercise.

15 to 30 minutes daily exercise is compulsory for parts of your body.

Take daily diets having vitamins and minerals, Vitamins and minerals improve your metabolic activities, they keep your body in good condition. Phytonutrients are also very important. Take raw foods such as vegetables suitable to you.

Yes, you may want to know what about me! Right I love gardening, I do gardening and a little exercise. You know I'm diabetic, heart and asthma patient. I take medicines. I take AMWAY multivitamins and raw vegetables. It keeps me my health in good conditions.

Now, what about the poor, yes your goal is your best things. If there is a will there is a way, don't forget this.

Take cheaper multivitamins first, frequently. Then replace them by organically manufactured vitamins and minerals.

Make your health good. If you are strong and healthy you will be able to concentrate on your goals. Do exercise, why not you; Be brave. Overcome your fear, be on the win. I want to see you healthy and success.

Meditate daily 10 minutes. You will feel new Experience. It is your duty to keep yourself happy and healthy.

I want to say good foods and walking is the best for your health. It also includes healthy body, sound mind. Sound mind, healthy body.

In the journey of success a good sound mind can produce good amount of creativity.

Chapter - V

CREATIVITY

Create plus activity is equal to creativity.

It is also very important part in your journey of success. Meditation activity makes you creativity. It brings you creative ideas. When you put informations in your mind your conscious mind receives it. When you repeat thinking all problems and informations your conscious mind receives it and have stored the inputs into your subconscious mind. Your subconscious mind ceaselessly work for you day and night.

As things change quickly, so adapt the change. Your creativity will make you possible to adapt this change.

Don't stop asking everyday why and what and how.

Hold a paper and a pen always with you. When sudden flash of ideas, solutions come up in your mind, write them down. Don't allow to slip them away by thinking that you shall write it later. It is because you cannot recall it anytime when you need it.

It is you who should give ideas and solutions to your future generations.

There is a story that a wise and very intelligent rich king was there once. He thought of something to do for the future of men and people. He announced a price that would enticed everyone of his men. He said, "Bring me the knowledge which contains all wisdom of all ages for which they will get this reward". All wise men tried by writing a voluminous book that contains all wisdom of all ages. The king said. "It is too long, try to condense it." Then the wise men discussed and wrote the book into small book. But the king again rejected. They tried it again and brought it to the king in three pages. The wise king said . "It is still long. nobody will read it in full." the wise men again condensed all knowledge of all ages in one paragraph and submitted it to the king. But the king pursued to condense it more so that it may be a slogan. They again wrote the knowledge of all ages into one sentence. " It is "there is No Free Meal in Life."

The wise king satisfied at his intelligent, creative men and gave the reward.

Creativity needs more, more experiments, more informations. Human mind can conceive whatever he wants. It is you to think and bring out your inner potential by putting more whys and hows into your mind.

So, hold a piece of paper and when sudden flash of ideas emerges out, write it down. But never forget your success. Such your ideas you have should be relating with your profession.

See new things, new videos, how the ideas are created, read books then your inner world will work for you. Don't try outside only.

There is another story about journey, which instead of inside journey. This is the story-a rich man was covetous for wealth. He heard about diamond and its value. He also heard that diamond was abundantly found in Africa. So he sold all his land to his neighbour. He went in search of diamond with some of his retinues.

He went and went on through jungles very long. He never reached the diamond land. And some of his retinues died on the way and some refused to go. Then he alone wanted to go further in search of diamond. Then, he went alone. At last he found a very high hill. He could not go further. And he had no way to return. He died there.

On the other hand, the man who bought the land from that greedy person, oneday found a lump of diamond in his field. He asked what it was to his friends. Then he came to know it was diamond and the field was diamond field.

He collected diamonds from that field and sold it to the diamond sellers. In that village he became the richest man. He also helped poor people and lived happily.

The story goes that greedy goes to grave and the diamond is within you as you see the diamond was found in sold land. Again greedy never works. The diamond is within you. Discover diamond from yourself, within yourself. Your inner can create unlimited ideas. Tape it, create and earn money.

Yes, it is really what to extract from within. It's really difficult to understand and know what your really want in life because there are unlimited wants for your, But find it. Do it what you feel joy when doing it.

I had many wants, but wants are unlimited. Some of them I can get. But in pursuing to get all wants I become a mediocre.

Now, find what you really want in life to become rich and successful you need to choose two or three wants as your goal. This is your profession. Then pursue it.

Chapter - VI

PROFESSION

As a businessman I focus mainly on business. I say however, the above chapters (Principles) are all applicable in areas of life and trades, jobs.

Now, you see, it is difficult to understand and know what you really want in life, a chosen profession. It is difficult to choose your proper profession because you are talented in many area of works.

So I suggest you to find one or two or three profession. Limit to it.

Now why you need a profession it is because without profession, you cannot earn and enjoy life.

In "Acorn Principle" by Jim Cathcart, he suggests how to choose your right profession. You have two profiles of your own. The 1st is external profile of you, your name, location, educational qualification etc.

Internal profile is your habits, your work pace, your favourite work and your suitable work time - morning, evening or night. What you value most, You intensity in work say- some like work as play and some like to work seriously.

These will be helpful in choosing your profession.

Someone who likes to be a doctor but external pressure he got to do engineering. Yes, he was good. But he could not be popular as an Engineer.

Do whatever profession you like most. It may cobbler, painting, singer, doctor, engineer etc. as you like.

My profession is business in jewellery and Industry. But my most like work is painting. I am also painter, I practice it from my childhood. Now I have abandoned painting. But still I use my creative painting in my jewellery design production.

Before, I took up my business I choose many trades such as clothes shops I failed, I choose micro finance I failed, I choose air ticketing, train, bus ticketing, I failed.

I started grocery items selling I failed.

It was tough time for my existence. I also went schools and college as teaching profession. I failed. Everything was not a total failure. It is the money I cannot reach from that jobs to maintain my life and to have a marriage.

The last option was jewellery business. I started by a little money. I continue jewellery business. I become a successful person, but successful in the sense I am abundant. But not very rich or richest man.

So never recognise failure. Every one of you will face problems and failures. It is who abandon trying who fails. Tough time never last but tough people do.

Your profession is your life. You can profess any lines such as writer, musician, sportsman, Govt. Jobs, business person etc.

Your profession is what you do it with happiness. Work done with happiness is more productive. Find your profession as you choose good and feel happy. Suitable profession makes you earn more and get promoted to high rank and bring you to fame.

You can do - A new venture as I was doing, corona preventive medicine (during pandemic) Herbal Asthma medicines, herbal mosquito repellent, Fish Farming, ginger Planting, Bee Keeping, Organic Manure, diabetic herbal medicines and many more. Tough time never last, Only tough people do.

Chapter –VII:

FAME

Fame is naturally followed by what you have worked and works for the people. The more you get, give the more. You give the more you will get the more. You are not born to eat, to live and die. You are born, you are meant to be something, you, should know you are highly valuable.

Any work you do, should be done with the idea of serving people, would you ?

Magician gives enjoyment with wonders to the audiences. Singer gives ecstasy to the hearer. Comedian makes laughs to all.

Fame automatically comes when you grow rich so serve the people.

Charlie Chaplin was famous comedian. He acted comedy scene with acting. He was rich and famous but died a broke.

Anyway habits on ethical lines is best for fame and prosperity.

You are known by your habits, good or bad. Bad habits brings you down. Good habits bring you rise.

Habits of giving, habits of loving, will define you, your success and rich.

Chapter - VIII

SAVING

Habits of saving is one of the element for success. You may face hard times. Saving makes you safe. Saving is very important as we need money for existing a good and happy life. Success is a journey not a destination.

Every success has some set back. To encounter such unwanted challenges you need some reserved money.

Is that right ? Yes. So, Save money for your future progress.

Now I would like to suggest you some forms money saving.

You can save money in banks.

I did all these kind of savings. I had many saving accounts. I sometimes forget that I have saved some money in the banks. True !when you need money you will check everything.

At last ! Aha ! now I have some money on these or that banks.

Ok, another type of saving for the purpose of your business is Marup. I call this Marup. It is really being practiced by our local people.

Marup means a system in which we organise a group of people from my friends, family and neighbours. The group may consist of 10 people or 20 people and more. It is done according to our convenience. I suggest you the more people in the group it is likely to break the Marup before completion. So we make at least 10 to 20 people in the group.

In Marup, for example, a group of twenty (20) people, each individual contributes some amount of money equally. Say Rs. 1000/- (One thousand per person). The total money is Rs. 20,000/- (Twenty thousands).

Then who will get the total money ?

Generally, the person who organises the Marup takes the first turn.

Then, who will get the 2nd turn ? The Answer is - The organiser makes a serial list. According to the serial of names like first, 2nd, 3rd .... so on.

According to this serial list, the person on his/her turn will get the Marup money. The serial goes on till the completion of 20 people. The serial Marup is done monthly. So it takes 20 months to complete the Marup.

If it is for 10 (ten) people Marup. It takes only 10 (ten) months.

Remember, from the 2nd to the last turn each individual in the Marup will pay monthly minimum amount interest one thousand along with their contribution money (Rs. 1,000) plus interest. Say for example, 2nd person who got the Marup pays Rs. 1000 + Rs. 50 (Rs. 1,050) till the completion of the Marup. All individuals except the organizer of the Marup will pay their contribution along with interest.

Picture - Organizer - will get Rs. 20000; 2nd person - will get Rs. 20000; 3rd person - will get Rs. 20,000 + Rs. 50 + Rs. 50,th person will get Rs. 20,000 + Rs. 50 + Rs. 50 + Rs. 50. It goes on till the completion of the marup.

The organizer receives first and he/she is exempted from interest payment because he/she manages the marup and take all responsibility of the Marup.

Next, another type of Marup is by Lottery. In this, the first turn is for the organizer. The rest will be chosen from the lottery. It is done every month till the completion of the Marup.

These are the examples of saving money being practiced in our community. So, think and do different way for saving money. Remember, money comes quickly it goes away quickly. So the way you use the money that makes your happy or Sad.

As important as saving, health, profession inner strength in the journey of success and happy life, time is the most important element.

Chapter - IX

TIME MANAGEMENT

Profession may be changed, lost health can be regained but lost time never return. Everything exists on time. Only time exists, nothing is permanent except time.

So, it is so precious, make your time so sweet, spend time almost with happy moments. We are born for success and happiness. By using time properly you will be elevated to high position and eventually the Fame for you.

In a day we get 24 hours in which we divide two parts One is sleeping time and the 2nd is waking.

Sleep will 6 to 7 hours a day, it is best for your health and mind.

The rest is waking hours, it is 17 hours we get.

There are two different ways how we use time. One is quality time spending and two, is low quality time spending time or unproductive time use.

For success and happiness we need to spend quality time. But I will not mention low quality time spending.

How to spend quality time - spend your time with joy. Engage your mind in something productive. Productive means spiritually and materially and physically.

Engage in work like painting, singing, writing, gardening, kitchen dish preparing, walking, gathering with friends and family. Social works, meditation, outing and tourist also refresh our mind and many more.

Remember our mind and body cannot always be kept in joy. Joy is your dominant state of existence, less sadness is part of your life.

Set your plan for every day's work in the written form. Try to implement your daily work for the day. Never mind if you wouldn't complete your work. Ok, you appreciate for the work done to yourself. "I am happy, I am happy, I thank myself for this work I have done to day". You have been successful for these works that you have done, why not you appreciate it ! Appreciation has tremendous value.

Practice this regularly, then later, you will be able to accomplish whatever work under hand. A brisk rest is required.

Above this is a brief sketch of what I do.

There is no free time for me because I engage in something like kitchen gardening reading book, seeing videos.

These are besides my business works.

Adjust your time according to your convenience.

Time destroys, time heals.

There is no question of age. Age is considered a number. If you are healthy everything is possible.

Go with a big dream. Happiness lies there in, the journey of happy life.

CONCLUSION

Don't think I am all in all. Knowledge is so vast. Everyday things are changing, you are changing, we are changing so knowledge is also changing. I share what I know only. I just share this only to help people. It is not for personal gain. But I know one thing that fame is followed naturally from the work and dedication done by one to people.

Happiness does not mean you should be a big officer, or a richest man, to be an engineer, a doctor or a scientists. It means fulfillment of you what you are gifted with, by enjoying it also means you to be abundant.

All subjects discussed in chapter wise are inter-related and inter-connected and the lack of one element you will feel imperfect and less joy.

Finance is very important. Financially when you are free but lack of health will lead you to uncomfortable life. Same is true for your profession also and you need certain amount of good health.

Enjoy your money when you are financially free. Financial freedom doesn't mean you do whatever you want. There should be some restrain.

It is your inner strength base on morality and ethics. This will give you joy, when you use your money.

As I said previously the more you give, the more you get. It is true, nature is abundant, it will return directly or indirectly from many sources when you give money with your good motive that without expecting for return.

You are really born for something. Find it and do it. Get out of your homeostatic conditions. You will be successful. Naturally your fame will follow. Action is primary and fame is not to be pursued.

Life is always up and down. Save money for your downtime. It is you and what you are by the way how you use your money.

Start, just today, time is limited for you make goals after goals. Divide times according to your goals and your convenience.

On my next book. I will share how to start up your business. If you are rich or poor, from where you are whether high or low, you can.

Remember, you are already abundant. It is the question of only you to take it out of you, from your within.

Don't confuse, now manage yourself by remembering the above principles.

People want to live happily. But in seeking happiness they go on the wrong path. My little book is not my own imagination. Ideas and saying are from books and my own experience. All motivational books have similar elements. I found it as I had read hundreds of books on motivations for success and happiness.

So seven elements for getting success and happiness are really of prime importance in our journey, at WHERE YOU ARE.

Definitely, great and successful rich people possess these seven elements. They practiced it. They got it.

Yes, I practice it. I failed. I start again and I failed again. But I am resilient. Now I am successful and abundant.

In the 2nd volume, on the next publication I will elaborately discuss how to start up your business, and what business is suitable for you, your options in business.

Being a businessman I touch only working and earning side. But I don't ignore govt. jobs.

I mainly inspire those who are under 20 p.e. of world's rich people. I want to elevate them to richness.

I thank a lot the Blue Rose Publishers for supporting me and inspiring me, motivating me. So that I am able to share my experience in business to people. Thanks

Author's Name :

Ningthoujam Basanta Singh

ABOUT THE BOOK

So seven elements for getting success and happiness are really of prime importance in our journey, at WHERE YOU ARE!

Definitely, great and successful rich people possess these seven elements. They practiced it. They got it.

Yes, I practice it. I failed. I start again and I failed again. But I am resilient. Now I am successful and abundant.

In the 2nd volume, on the next publication I will elaborately discuss how to start up your business, and what business is suitable for you, your options in business.

Being a businessman I touch only working and earning side. But I don't ignore govt. jobs.

I mainly inspire those who are under 20 p.e. of world's rich people. I want to elevate them to richness.

I thank a lot the Blue Rose Publishers for supporting me and inspiring me, motivating me. So that I am able to share my experience in business to people. Thanks

Author's Name :

Ningthoujam Basanta Singh

www.ingramcontent.com/pod-product-compliance
Lightning Source LLC
LaVergne TN
LVHW041600070526
838199LV00046B/2072